12 Nights of Holiday Magic

12 Nights of Holiday Magic

Matthew Petchinsky

12 Nights of Holiday Magic
By: Matthew Petchinsky

Introduction: The Countdown to Magic

In the heart of the holiday season, when snow blankets the earth in a serene hush and the world feels touched by an ethereal glow, there lies an age-old tradition that holds the promise of wonder and magic. These are the 12 nights leading up to Christmas—a sacred time steeped in folklore, whispered secrets, and ancient enchantments. For centuries, people have believed that during these nights, the veil between the ordinary and the extraordinary thins, allowing the miraculous to slip into the lives of the deserving.

Nestled amidst a frost-covered forest stands the small town of Evergreen Hollow, a place seemingly plucked from a snow globe. Here, traditions run deep, and tales of magic are shared with reverence around crackling fires. It is said that Evergreen Hollow is home to the legendary "Magic Calendar," an artifact of breathtaking mystery and power. Passed down through generations, the Magic Calendar is no ordinary holiday decoration. This mystical artifact grants a singular, enchanted gift each night to those fortunate enough to unlock its secrets.

The origin of the Magic Calendar is shrouded in mystery. Some say it was crafted by the hands of the Northern Lights themselves, forged in a realm where time and magic intertwine. Others believe it was a gift from Father Christmas to the people of the town, a reward for their unwavering faith in the spirit of the season. Regardless of its origins, one thing remains certain: the Magic Calendar has transformed lives, weaving its magic into the fabric of Evergreen Hollow's history.

Each night, as the clock strikes midnight, the calendar reveals a hidden compartment containing a magical token. These tokens are no mere trinkets—they are imbued with extraordinary powers, granting the bearer abilities that defy the laws of nature. From the power to heal the weary to the ability to summon warmth in the coldest storms, each gift mirrors the essence of the holiday spirit, inspiring generosity, courage, and love.

But with great magic comes an even greater mystery. Rumors swirl that the Magic Calendar is more than just a giver of gifts—it is a guide, a map to a hidden truth that only the bravest and most determined can uncover. Some believe that those who complete its 12-night journey will discover a treasure that transcends wealth, unlocking the key to an enduring kind of happiness.

As snowflakes fall silently in Evergreen Hollow, painting the town in shades of silver and white, the stage is set for a tale unlike any other. This is a story of a chosen few who embark on a quest to claim the calendar's gifts, only to find themselves caught in an adventure where the stakes are as high as the stars above. It is a story of mystery and wonder, of facing fears and embracing the unknown, all against the backdrop of the most magical season of all.

Welcome to the Countdown to Magic. Let the journey begin.

Chapter 1: The Magic Calendar's Arrival

The attic of their grandmother's house was a treasure trove of memories. Dust motes danced in the faint golden light streaming through the single circular window, and the air was thick with the smell of aged wood and mothballs. For siblings Mia and Oliver, the attic was an irresistible maze of old trunks, forgotten knick-knacks, and mysterious heirlooms. It was a place where adventure was as certain as the snow that blanketed Evergreen Hollow in December.

This year, with Christmas just weeks away, Mia and Oliver found themselves exploring the attic while their grandmother prepared cookies downstairs. The pair had been tasked with retrieving a box of Christmas ornaments, but they were quickly distracted by an ornate chest tucked away in the far corner.

"Mia, look at this," Oliver said, brushing off a layer of dust. The chest was unlike anything they had ever seen. Its exterior was carved with intricate patterns of stars, snowflakes, and holly leaves. At the center of the lid was an engraving of a calendar with twelve tiny doors, each marked with a number from 1 to 12.

"This doesn't look like the usual stuff up here," Mia murmured, running her fingers over the engraving. "It's beautiful."

Curiosity got the better of them, and with a creak, they opened the chest. Inside was the calendar itself—large, gilded, and glowing faintly as if it were alive. It wasn't just a picture or a carving; this was a three-dimensional object with real, tiny doors embedded into it. The craftsmanship was extraordinary. Each door seemed to shimmer with its own unique pattern, as though holding a secret waiting to be revealed.

Mia and Oliver exchanged a glance. Something about the calendar felt significant, almost sacred.

"Should we take it downstairs?" Oliver asked hesitantly.

Mia shook her head. "Let's look at it first. Grandma can wait for the ornaments."

As soon as Mia touched the calendar, the room seemed to change. A faint hum filled the air, and the light from the attic window grew brighter. Suddenly, a folded note slipped out from the back of the calendar and landed softly on the floor.

Oliver picked it up, unfolding the parchment carefully. The handwriting was elegant and looping, and the message sent a shiver down their spines.

To the Bearers of the Magic Calendar,
This artifact holds the power of holiday magic. Each night, at the stroke of midnight, a door will open, revealing a gift or challenge meant to prepare you for the greatest task of all.
But beware: the calendar's magic is not eternal. Its gifts must be completed and its challenges overcome by Christmas Eve, or the magic in Evergreen Hollow will vanish forever.
Guard its power, and let its magic guide you.

"What does that mean?" Oliver whispered, his voice barely audible.

"I don't know," Mia said, her eyes fixed on the calendar. "But I think we're supposed to find out."

That night, as the clock struck midnight, Mia and Oliver sat cross-legged in their grandmother's living room, the Magic Calendar placed carefully between them. The first door, numbered with a gold *1*, began to glow. Slowly, the tiny door creaked open, revealing a miniature snowflake charm that sparkled like the morning frost.

As soon as Mia reached out to touch it, the charm dissolved into a burst of light that enveloped them both. The room filled with the sound of jingling bells, soft laughter, and the warm hum of holiday cheer. When the light faded, Mia and Oliver looked at each other, wide-eyed.

"What just happened?" Oliver asked.

Before either of them could answer, they noticed something extraordinary. The once-dim living room now glowed with a warmth that seemed to emanate from them. The Christmas tree sparkled brighter, the fireplace crackled more invitingly, and even the air smelled of cinnamon and pine.

A strange sense of joy bubbled up inside Mia, so strong she couldn't help but laugh. "I think... I think it's us. We're making everything feel like Christmas!"

Testing her theory, Mia stood up and walked toward the kitchen, Oliver close behind. Wherever they moved, the warmth and cheer followed. Their grandmother, who had been quietly decorating cookies, looked up and smiled.

"It feels so festive in here," she said. "I don't know what it is, but it's wonderful."

Mia and Oliver exchanged a knowing glance. It was the calendar.

As the night wore on, the glow faded, but the siblings knew it was only the beginning. The Magic Calendar had chosen them for a reason. Its gifts were not just random acts of magic; they were pieces of a puzzle, each one leading to something greater.

But the warning in the note lingered in their minds. If they failed to unlock the calendar's magic by Christmas Eve, Evergreen Hollow's holiday magic would be lost forever.

"We can't mess this up," Mia said firmly as they returned the calendar to its resting place for the night.

Oliver nodded, his expression serious. "We'll figure it out. One door at a time."

With that, the siblings went to bed, their hearts filled with a mix of excitement and determination. The Magic Calendar had come into their lives, and with it, a challenge that would test their courage, their bond, and their belief in the power of holiday magic.

Chapter 2: The Snowflake Keeper

As the clock struck midnight on the second night, the Magic Calendar came alive once more. Mia and Oliver had been waiting anxiously, sitting beside the glowing artifact in their grandmother's living room. The second door, marked with a shimmering silver *2*, began to glimmer like moonlight on freshly fallen snow.

"Ready?" Mia whispered, though her voice betrayed her nervous excitement.

Oliver nodded, reaching out to touch the tiny silver door. As his fingers grazed it, the door opened, releasing a burst of icy wind that swirled around the room. The siblings clung to each other as the living room faded, replaced by a landscape of breathtaking wonder.

They stood in a dazzling, crystalline world. Snowflakes the size of their hands drifted gently from a sky shimmering with auroras. The ground sparkled like a carpet of diamonds, and towering ice sculptures reflected the soft glow of the magical sky. Yet this beauty was tempered by a sense of fragility, as if the entire realm could shatter with a careless touch.

"Where are we?" Oliver asked, his breath visible in the frigid air.

Before Mia could answer, a figure emerged from the swirling snow. It was a tall, ethereal being cloaked in robes that seemed to be woven from frost itself. Her face was ageless and serene, her hair cascading like icicles down her shoulders. In her hands, she carried a staff crowned with a glowing snowflake.

"I am the Snowflake Keeper," she said, her voice as soft as falling snow but tinged with urgency. "You are the chosen bearers of the Magic Calendar. I have been waiting for you."

Mia and Oliver exchanged uneasy glances. "Why are we here?" Mia asked.

The Snowflake Keeper gestured toward the vast, shimmering land-scape. "This is the Realm of Living Snowflakes, where every snowflake in your world is born. Each flake carries its own unique magic, a delicate balance that preserves the beauty and harmony of winter. But our realm is in danger."

"What kind of danger?" Oliver asked, stepping closer.

The Snowflake Keeper's serene expression darkened. "The Snowflake Queen's crown has been stolen. Without it, the balance of winter's magic is breaking. Snow will turn to ice storms, beauty to chaos. The thief is a Frost Imp, driven by jealousy of the Queen's power. You must retrieve the crown before it is too late."

Mia felt a pang of fear. "Why us? We're just... kids."

The Snowflake Keeper placed a cold yet comforting hand on Mia's shoulder. "The Magic Calendar has chosen you for a reason. You possess the courage, creativity, and kindness needed to restore what has been lost. But this task will not be easy."

Before the siblings could ask more questions, the Keeper waved her staff, and a portal of swirling frost appeared.

"Go now. The Frost Imp lurks in the Ice Caverns to the north. But be warned: his trickery is as dangerous as the ice itself."

With a deep breath, Mia and Oliver stepped through the portal, finding themselves in a dark, glittering cavern. The walls sparkled with frost, but the air was heavy with an ominous chill.

"I don't like this," Oliver muttered, his breath fogging in the cold air.

Mia nodded. "Let's stick together."

As they ventured deeper, the cavern twisted and turned, revealing shimmering stalactites and pools of icy water. In the distance, a flickering blue light caught their attention.

"That must be him," Mia whispered, gripping Oliver's arm.

They approached cautiously, and there, perched atop a jagged ice throne, was the Frost Imp. He was small, with sharp features and skin that glowed faintly like frozen glass. The Snowflake Queen's crown rested on his head, its delicate crystals glowing faintly.

"Well, well," the Imp sneered, his voice echoing eerily. "What do we have here? Little mortals, sent to steal my treasure?"

"It's not yours!" Oliver said, stepping forward. "The crown belongs to the Snowflake Queen!"

The Imp laughed, a sound like cracking ice. "Belongs to her? Why should she have all the power? This crown is mine now, and there's nothing you can do about it."

Mia stepped beside her brother, her mind racing. The Imp was too fast and too clever to confront directly. They needed a plan.

"Maybe we don't have to fight him," she whispered to Oliver. "Maybe we can trick him."

Oliver frowned. "How?"

Mia thought for a moment, then reached into her pocket, pulling out the snowflake charm they had received the previous night. It still glimmered faintly, a reminder of their newfound ability to summon holiday cheer.

"I have an idea," she said.

She stepped forward, holding the charm high. "Hey, Imp!" she called. "You think that crown is powerful? It's nothing compared to this."

The Imp's eyes widened, drawn to the glowing charm. "What is that?"

"It's pure holiday magic," Mia said confidently. "With it, you could have more power than the Snowflake Queen ever dreamed of."

The Imp's greed flared, and he leapt from his throne, reaching for the charm. But as he did, Mia tossed it to Oliver, who darted behind the throne.

"Catch me if you can!" Oliver shouted, running in circles around the cavern.

The Imp gave chase, his focus entirely on the charm. In his haste, he discarded the crown, which Mia quickly snatched up.

"Got it!" she yelled.

The Imp froze, realizing he had been outwitted. "You tricked me!" he screeched.

"Let's go!" Mia shouted, grabbing Oliver's hand. Together, they ran back toward the portal, the Imp's furious cries echoing behind them.

As they emerged back in the Realm of Living Snowflakes, the Snowflake Keeper was waiting. When she saw the crown, her face lit with relief.

"You have done well," she said, placing the crown back on her head. The realm seemed to shimmer brighter, the fragile balance of magic restored.

"What about the Imp?" Oliver asked, still catching his breath.

"He will trouble us no more," the Keeper said. "Your courage and cleverness have saved us."

As a final gift, the Keeper touched the calendar, causing it to glow softly.

"Your journey is far from over," she said. "But tonight, you have proven that even the most delicate beauty is worth protecting. Go now, and let the calendar guide you."

As Mia and Oliver stepped back into their grandmother's living room, the snowflake charm reappeared in Mia's hand, glowing faintly once more. The siblings knew that their adventure had only just begun, but they also knew they could face whatever lay ahead—together.

Chapter 3: The Holly Sprig of Hope

As midnight neared on the third night, Mia and Oliver once again gathered around the Magic Calendar. The previous nights had filled them with equal parts excitement and trepidation. Though they had triumphed twice, each challenge seemed to test them more than the last. The third door, adorned with an intricate carving of holly leaves and berries, began to glow softly.

"Ready for another adventure?" Mia asked, trying to sound braver than she felt.

Oliver hesitated for a moment before nodding. "Let's do this."

When the door opened, a faint green light emerged, accompanied by the faint scent of pine and earth. A folded parchment fell from the compartment, and Mia quickly picked it up. The note read:

"In the heart of the forest, beneath the ancient boughs,
Lies a tree of holly with power to arouse.
But its magic is fading, its light growing dim,
Restore the sprig, or hope shall not win."

Before they could ponder the riddle further, the room seemed to dissolve around them. They found themselves standing in the middle of a dense forest, bathed in the silver light of the full moon. Snow clung to the towering trees, and the air was crisp with the scent of winter.

"Where are we this time?" Oliver whispered, turning in circles to take in their surroundings.

Mia pointed ahead, where a faint golden glow pulsed between the trees. "I think we're supposed to go that way."

As they approached the light, the forest grew quieter, as though it were holding its breath. Finally, they emerged into a small clearing dominated by an ancient holly tree. Its gnarled trunk was enormous, and its branches stretched high into the sky, adorned with glossy green leaves and clusters of bright red berries. But the golden glow came from a hollow in its trunk, where a soft light flickered faintly.

"It's beautiful," Mia said, stepping closer.

But as they approached, the light dimmed, and a deep, sorrowful voice echoed through the clearing. "Who disturbs the Holly Tree of Hope?"

The siblings froze, and from the shadows emerged a figure no taller than Mia's knee. It was a wood sprite, with bark-like skin and hair made of moss and twigs. His face was etched into a permanent scowl, and he carried a tiny staff adorned with a single red berry.

"I am Thorn, guardian of this tree," he said gruffly. "And if you're here to take from it, you'd best turn around."

"We're here to help," Oliver said quickly. "The Magic Calendar sent us. We need to restore the holly's sprig."

Thorn narrowed his eyes. "Why should I believe you? Everyone comes here wanting something. They care nothing for the tree or what it gives. They only want its wishes."

Mia knelt to meet Thorn's gaze. "We don't want to take anything. We want to help. Please tell us what's wrong."

The sprite hesitated, his scowl softening slightly. "The tree is dying," he admitted. "Its magic comes from the holly sprig, a sacred branch that grants hope to those who nurture it. But the sprig has been stolen. Without it, the tree's light fades, and so does the hope it spreads to the world."

"Do you know who took it?" Oliver asked.

Thorn sighed. "A fox spirit, sly and greedy, tricked me and ran off with the sprig. I tried to chase it, but I lost its trail in the forest. Without the sprig, the tree will wither completely by dawn."

"We'll find it," Mia said firmly.

Thorn scoffed. "You? Two human children? The forest is vast, and the fox is cunning. What makes you think you can succeed where I failed?"

"We'll find a way," Oliver said. "Because we have to."

The sprite studied them for a long moment, then reluctantly nodded. "Very well. If you're determined to try, I'll help as I can. But beware: the fox spirit will not give up the sprig willingly."

The Riddle of the Forest

With Thorn leading the way, the siblings set off into the forest. The trees seemed to grow taller and darker as they ventured deeper, their branches forming a canopy that blocked out the moonlight. Thorn explained that the fox spirit loved riddles and would only return the sprig if they solved one of its puzzles.

After what felt like hours of searching, they found the fox spirit lounging on a snow-covered rock in a clearing. Its fur shimmered like starlight, and its eyes gleamed with mischief. Around its neck hung the stolen holly sprig, glowing faintly.

"Well, well," the fox said, its voice smooth and melodic. "Visitors. And here I thought the Holly Tree had been forgotten."

"We're here to get the sprig back," Mia said boldly.

The fox tilted its head, amused. "Oh? And why should I give it to you? This sprig is precious, and I quite like it as my trophy."

"Because the tree needs it to survive," Oliver said.

The fox yawned lazily. "What do I care for the tree? Its time has passed."

Mia clenched her fists. "Please. We'll do whatever it takes."

The fox's eyes sparkled with amusement. "Very well. If you can solve my riddle, I'll return the sprig. But if you fail, I'll keep it forever."

The siblings nodded, their hearts pounding.

The fox grinned and recited:

"I am not alive, but I can grow.
I have no lungs, but I need air.
I have no mouth, and yet I roar.
What am I?"

Mia and Oliver exchanged panicked glances, the words echoing in their minds.

"It's... it's a fire!" Oliver blurted out after a moment.

The fox's grin faltered, and it let out a low growl. "Clever little mortals," it said, removing the sprig from its neck. "You have bested me. Take your precious sprig."

Mia reached out and took the holly sprig carefully. The moment she touched it, a wave of warmth and light spread through the clearing. The fox vanished in a swirl of snow, leaving only a faint chuckle behind.

Restoring Hope

Back at the Holly Tree, Thorn was waiting anxiously. When the siblings returned the sprig to the hollow, the tree glowed brighter than ever. Its leaves sparkled like emeralds, and its berries shone like rubies.

"You've done it," Thorn said, his voice filled with wonder.

The tree's magic washed over the forest, filling it with warmth and light. Thorn's grumpy demeanor melted away, replaced by genuine gratitude.

"Thank you," he said quietly. "For caring enough to help. I see now that hope isn't just something the tree gives—it's something we nurture in each other."

As the siblings returned to their grandmother's house, the holly sprig appeared on the calendar, now glowing softly as a reminder of their success. Mia and Oliver fell asleep that night with a renewed sense of purpose, ready for whatever challenge the Magic Calendar would bring next.

Chapter 4: The Star of Reunion

The soft chime of the clock striking midnight sent a familiar shiver of anticipation through Mia and Oliver. By now, the Magic Calendar had become a centerpiece of their holiday nights, a gateway to adventures more extraordinary than they could have imagined. Tonight, the fourth door—etched with intricate patterns of swirling stars—began to glow with a silver light.

"What do you think it'll be this time?" Oliver asked, sitting cross-legged on the floor beside his sister.

"Only one way to find out," Mia said, gently opening the glowing door.

From within, a silver light spilled out, illuminating the room. A tiny star-shaped charm floated out, spinning slowly in the air before settling in Mia's palm. The room seemed to fade as a soothing voice filled the space around them.

"To the Starry Way, where light is lost and found. Guide the stars, and hearts will be mended."

The voice dissolved into silence, and the siblings were suddenly enveloped in light. When the brilliance dimmed, they found themselves standing in a vast, cosmic expanse. Above and around them stretched the Starry Way—a glittering bridge of starlight arching across an endless void. The air was cool and crisp, filled with the faint hum of celestial music.

"Where are we?" Oliver whispered, gazing in awe at the endless stars around them.

Mia pointed ahead, where a cluster of stars shimmered faintly, as if calling for help. "I think we're supposed to go there."

Meeting the Lost Stars

As they stepped onto the Starry Way, the shimmering light beneath their feet felt solid yet soft, like walking on a cloud. When they reached the cluster of dim stars, a figure appeared before them—a celestial being, translucent and glowing, with hair that flowed like silver ribbons and eyes that held the entire night sky.

"I am Astra, Keeper of the Starry Way," the being said, her voice gentle and melodic. "You have been sent to help the lost stars find their way back to the Christmas Constellation."

"Lost stars?" Mia asked, tilting her head.

Astra nodded. "These stars are fragments of hope, joy, and love—gifts that were lost when families drifted apart. Some were separated by distance, others by disagreement. Without them, the Christmas Constellation cannot shine, and its magic will fade."

"What do we have to do?" Oliver asked.

Astra extended a hand, and a glowing map of the Starry Way appeared in the air. "The stars are scattered, each carrying a story of separation. You must guide them back, but beware: the journey will test your understanding of forgiveness and the power of togetherness."

Mia and Oliver exchanged determined glances. "We'll do it," Mia said.

The Stories of Separation

The siblings followed Astra's map to the first star, which hovered dimly near the edge of the Starry Way. As they approached, the star pulsed weakly, and a vision unfolded before them. They saw an elderly woman sitting alone in a cozy but empty house, staring wistfully at a photograph of a young family.

"This star belongs to her," Astra explained. "She longs to see her children and grandchildren again, but pride and old arguments have kept them apart."

"How do we help her?" Mia asked.

"You must show her the path of forgiveness," Astra replied. "Help her remember the love that binds them."

Mia touched the star, and a warm light spread from her fingertips. The vision shifted, showing the woman reaching for a phone and dialing a number with trembling hands. The star's light grew brighter, and it floated upward, joining a glowing path leading to the Christmas Constellation.

"That wasn't so bad," Oliver said, smiling.

"Don't get too comfortable," Astra warned. "The next stars may require more effort."

The second star was tangled in a web of dark shadows. As the siblings freed it, another vision unfolded: two siblings arguing in a crowded kitchen, their words sharp and their faces filled with anger.

"This one's about a fight," Oliver murmured.

Mia nodded. "They need to find a way to talk to each other again."

As they held the star, they whispered words of encouragement, imagining the siblings reconciling. Slowly, the shadows dissolved, and the vision changed to show the two hugging, tears of relief on their faces. The star brightened and joined the constellation.

The Final Challenge

The last star was the dimmest of all, barely visible as it drifted far from the Starry Way. When they reached it, Astra's expression grew somber.

"This star belongs to a family separated by great distance," she said. "They each miss one another, but fear rejection if they reach out."

Mia touched the star, and a vision emerged: parents working tirelessly in a distant city, their young child cared for by an elderly relative in Evergreen Hollow. The parents longed to return but feared they wouldn't be welcomed back after leaving.

"What can we do?" Oliver asked, feeling the weight of the family's sadness.

Mia closed her eyes, focusing on the warmth of the star. "We remind them that love is stronger than fear."

As she spoke, the star began to glow faintly. The vision shifted to show the parents arriving home with tearful apologies and the child rushing into their arms. The star's light grew brighter and brighter until it shone like a beacon.

With the final star restored, the Christmas Constellation came alive, its intricate pattern lighting up the entire Starry Way. The void around them filled with warmth and a sense of profound peace.

The Lesson of Reunion

Astra smiled, her celestial form glowing brighter. "You have done well. By reuniting these stars, you have reminded them—and your-selves—that forgiveness and love are the true magic of the season."

As the siblings prepared to leave, Astra handed them a small silver star, its surface warm to the touch. "Keep this as a reminder of the power of bringing people together."

When they returned to their grandmother's living room, the silver star appeared on the Magic Calendar, glowing softly as a symbol of the night's lesson.

"I think this was the most important one yet," Mia said, placing the star carefully on a shelf.

Oliver nodded. "Yeah. If the stars can find their way back, so can peo-ple."

With that thought in their hearts, the siblings fell asleep, ready for the challenges and magic the next night would bring.

Chapter 5: The Final Door

The twelfth night had arrived, and with it came a sense of anticipation that filled Mia and Oliver's hearts. Over the past eleven nights, they had faced trials that tested their courage, wit, and compassion. They had gained gifts of magic, learned lessons of hope and forgiveness, and helped others in ways they never thought possible. Now, the final door on the Magic Calendar stood before them, its intricate carvings glowing with a golden light that seemed brighter and warmer than ever before.

"We've come so far," Mia whispered, running her fingers over the ornate number *12* etched into the door.

Oliver nodded. "Whatever this last challenge is, we're ready."

As Mia opened the door, a radiant light flooded the room. From the tiny compartment, a rolled parchment floated out, its edges shimmering like frost. Mia unrolled it carefully, and both siblings read the message aloud:

"The final task is upon you. To save the Christmas Spirit, you must use all that you have learned and all that you have gained. Bring joy to your town, unite its people, and rekindle the light of the season before the clock strikes midnight on Christmas Eve."

The room began to transform, the golden light enveloping everything. When it faded, Mia and Oliver found themselves standing in the center of Evergreen Hollow, their grandmother's house far behind them. The town square, usually bustling with holiday cheer, was eerily quiet. Snow fell softly, but the festive glow of Christmas lights was dim, and the laughter of children was absent.

"It feels... sad," Oliver said, shivering slightly.

Mia nodded. "It's like the Christmas Spirit is already fading. We need to act fast."

Planning the Grand Celebration

The siblings sat on a nearby bench, unrolling the parchment again for guidance. As they read the words, they realized the task wasn't just about performing a single magical act—it was about bringing the entire town together.

"We'll need to use everything," Mia said thoughtfully. "All the gifts, all the lessons. If we're going to save the Christmas Spirit, we need to remind everyone of what this season is really about."

Oliver looked around the quiet square. "So we organize a celebration. The biggest, most magical holiday event Evergreen Hollow has ever seen."

Mia grinned. "Exactly."

Using the Magic Gifts

The siblings began their preparations, calling on the gifts from previous nights.

- **The Cheer of the Snowflake Charm (Night 1):** With a wave of their hands, they spread holiday cheer throughout the square. Lights flickered to life, and snow began to glisten like diamonds. A warm, inviting glow spread through the streets, drawing curious townsfolk from their homes.
- **The Strength of the Holly Sprig (Night 3):** They placed the magical sprig at the center of the square, and its energy filled the town with hope and renewal. People who had been distant or grumpy felt their hearts soften, old grudges fading away.
- **The Guiding Light of the Stars (Night 4):** The siblings used the silver star from the Starry Way to create a breathtaking display of constellations in the night sky. The stars shimmered and danced, reminding everyone of the importance of unity and forgiveness.

As the townsfolk gathered, the siblings enlisted their help to create a truly memorable celebration. Together, they decorated trees, baked cookies, and strung garlands of holly and ivy. The joy of shared effort brought smiles and laughter, and soon the square was alive with the sounds of carols and the aroma of hot cocoa.

The Final Challenge

As the clock neared midnight, Mia and Oliver noticed a faint flicker in the center of the square. The Magic Calendar had appeared, its doors glowing softly. The parchment they had been carrying floated upward, dissolving into golden sparks.

"What's happening?" Oliver asked, clutching Mia's arm.

The Keeper of the Starry Way appeared, her celestial form radiant. "The Christmas Spirit is rekindling, but there is one final act you must complete," she said. "The spirit cannot thrive without a spark of true selflessness. You must offer something from yourselves to complete the magic."

The siblings exchanged uncertain glances. What could they give?

Mia looked at the silver star in her hand, then at the crowd of joyful faces around them. "I think I know."

She turned to Oliver. "It's the gifts. All of them. We have to give them back to the calendar."

"But what if we need them again?" Oliver asked hesitantly.

Mia smiled. "We don't. We've already learned everything they had to teach us. The magic isn't in the objects—it's in what we've done with them."

The Spark of Selflessness

One by one, Mia and Oliver placed the magical items back into the calendar: the snowflake charm, the holly sprig, the silver star, and every token they had collected on their journey. As each item returned, the calendar glowed brighter, its light filling the square and spreading outward like a wave.

The townsfolk watched in awe as the light enveloped them, warming their hearts and lifting their spirits. The clock struck midnight, and with a final burst of golden light, the calendar disappeared, leaving behind a single, glowing star that floated above the square.

The Keeper's voice echoed softly in the air. "The Christmas Spirit is restored, thanks to your courage, kindness, and selflessness. Evergreen Hollow will now shine as a beacon of holiday magic for generations to come."

A New Beginning

As the crowd erupted into cheers, Mia and Oliver felt a deep sense of accomplishment. They had done it—not just by using magic, but by bringing people together and reminding them of the true meaning of the season.

Their grandmother appeared, wrapping them in a warm embrace. "I don't know what you two have been up to, but this is the most magical Christmas Eve I've ever seen."

Mia and Oliver exchanged a smile, knowing they would never forget the incredible journey they had taken.

As the first notes of "Silent Night" filled the air, the glowing star above the square pulsed gently, a reminder that the Magic Calendar's gift was not just for one season, but for every Christmas to come.

Appendix A: The Lore of the Magic Calendar
Origins of the Magic Calendar

The Magic Calendar's history stretches back to an age when the boundaries between the magical and the mundane were more fluid. Legends speak of its creation by an ancient council of Winter Guardians—celestial beings entrusted with preserving the essence of holiday magic. These guardians, known as the Aurorans, sought to craft a powerful artifact that would embody the values of the season: joy, hope, forgiveness, and unity.

The Aurorans forged the Magic Calendar from starlight, holly wood, and enchanted frost gathered under the first full moon of winter. Each of its twelve doors was imbued with a specific magical lesson, designed to test and teach the bearers about the power of selflessness and the importance of bringing light into the darkest of times.

It is said that the calendar's creation coincided with the birth of the Christmas Constellation, a celestial formation that would only shine brightly when the true spirit of the season was alive in the hearts of those who celebrated it. The calendar served as both a safeguard for this spirit and a guide for those chosen to restore it when it began to wane.

The First Keepers

The Magic Calendar's first keeper was a humble woodcarver named Elias, who lived in a snowy village not unlike Evergreen Hollow. One winter, when a terrible storm threatened to destroy his town's livelihood, Elias discovered the calendar hidden in a hollow tree. Each night, it revealed to him a magical gift or challenge, helping him unite his community and rebuild what had been lost. By the time Christmas Eve arrived, Elias had inspired such profound joy and hope that the storm subsided, leaving the village stronger than before.

Elias became the first in a long line of keepers, each chosen during a time of great need. Over the centuries, the calendar passed through many hands:

- **Clara the Weaver (16th Century):** A widow who used the calendar's magic to bring her war-torn village back together.
- **Jonas the Sailor (18th Century):** A mariner who restored hope to a shipwrecked crew lost at sea.
- **Amara the Orphan (19th Century):** A young girl who used the calendar to bring warmth and joy to a cold, lonely town.

Each keeper left their mark on the calendar, adding to its lore and ensuring its lessons endured.

The Enchanted Doors

The Magic Calendar's twelve doors are the heart of its mystery. Each door represents a fundamental element of the holiday spirit, revealed through its unique magic. Below is a detailed account of each door's lesson:

1. **The Snowflake Charm of Cheer:** This door symbolizes the transformative power of joy, granting the ability to brighten any room and inspire happiness.
2. **The Portal to the Snowflake Realm:** Teaching that even fragile beauty must be protected, this door tests courage and compassion.
3. **The Holly Sprig of Hope:** A lesson in nurturing faith and restoring broken bonds.
4. **The Star of Reunion:** Highlighting the importance of unity and forgiveness, this door encourages reconnection.
5. **The Sleigh Bell of Kindness:** An unseen gift encouraging small acts of generosity to ripple outward.
6. **The Flame of Resilience:** Granting warmth and light in dark times, this door inspires perseverance.

7. **The Crystal Compass:** Offering guidance through uncertainty, it teaches trust in oneself and others.
8. **The Evergreen Heart:** A reminder of the enduring power of love and family, symbolized by an unwithering pine sprig.
9. **The Lantern of Wisdom:** Shining light on forgotten traditions and hidden truths, this door fosters understanding.
10. **The Frost Mirror:** Reflecting one's true self, it challenges bearers to confront their fears and embrace change.
11. **The Golden Ribbon:** Binding community and shared purpose, this door highlights collective strength.
12. **The Star of Selflessness:** The final door embodies the culmination of all lessons, requiring an act of pure generosity to rekindle the Christmas Spirit.

Each door's carvings are uniquely intricate, adorned with symbols that hint at its hidden challenge. For example, the Holly Sprig door is surrounded by delicate vines and berries, while the Star of Reunion's door is etched with constellations.

The Calendar's Magic

The Magic Calendar's power lies in its ability to connect people to the essence of the holiday season. Its magic is not meant to grant unlimited power or personal gain but to inspire selflessness, hope, and unity. Those who complete its challenges often find themselves changed, their hearts opened to the true meaning of the season.

The calendar is also tied to the Christmas Constellation. When its lessons are completed, the constellation shines brighter, spreading holiday magic across the world. However, if the calendar's magic is left unfinished, the constellation dims, and the season loses its luster.

Illustrations of the Magic Calendar

1. The Calendar Itself: The Magic Calendar is a masterpiece of craftsmanship. Its base is crafted from polished holly wood, its surface inlaid with shimmering starlight and frost patterns. Each door is outlined in gold and silver, with tiny hinges that glow faintly when touched.

2. The Snowflake Door: The first door is adorned with an intricate carving of snowflakes, each unique, swirling in an eternal winter breeze.

3. The Holly Door: The third door features a vivid depiction of a holly branch, its berries gleaming like rubies.

4. The Star Door: The fourth door is surrounded by constellations, their patterns etched in glowing silver lines.

5. The Final Door: The twelfth door is the most breathtaking, a celestial map carved into its surface. At its center, a brilliant star radiates light, symbolizing the culmination of the calendar's magic.

The Calendar's Legacy

Though its origins remain shrouded in legend, the Magic Calendar's purpose is clear: to restore the light of the season when darkness threatens to extinguish it. By passing through the hands of chosen keepers, it ensures that its lessons endure across generations.

As the Magic Calendar rests now in the heart of Evergreen Hollow, its glow serves as a reminder of what the season truly represents. It is not merely an artifact of power, but a guide to rekindle the magic of Christmas within every heart it touches.

Appendix B: The Twelve Gifts of Magic

The twelve gifts of the Magic Calendar are more than enchanted objects; they symbolize values and lessons that embody the true spirit of the holiday season. Each gift serves as a reminder of a deeper meaning, encouraging kindness, joy, unity, and selflessness. Here, we explore the symbolism behind these magical gifts and offer suggestions for incorporating their lessons into real-life celebrations.

1. The Snowflake Charm of Cheer

Symbolism: The Snowflake Charm represents the transformative power of joy and the ability to uplift others. Like snowflakes, no act of kindness is too small to make a difference.

Inspiration:

- *Lesson:* Spread joy wherever you go. A warm smile or a kind word can brighten someone's day.
- *Activity:* Create homemade snowflake decorations and gift them to friends or neighbors. Write a cheerful note on each one to share a bit of holiday magic.

2. The Portal to the Snowflake Realm

Symbolism: This gift teaches the importance of protecting fragile beauty, whether it's the natural world or the delicate emotions of those around us.

Inspiration:

- *Lesson:* Appreciate and care for what is precious.
- *Activity:* Take a nature walk and collect snow or pinecones to create a simple centerpiece. Discuss with your family how to protect the environment during the holidays.

3. The Holly Sprig of Hope

Symbolism: The Holly Sprig represents resilience and hope, even in challenging times. Its evergreen nature reminds us that hope endures through all seasons.

Inspiration:

- *Lesson:* Nurture hope in yourself and others.
- *Activity:* Plant a small evergreen tree or holly bush as a family tradition. Decorate it with ribbons or ornaments symbolizing hopes for the coming year.

4. The Star of Reunion

Symbolism: This gift highlights the importance of unity and reconciliation, particularly during the holidays. Like stars returning to a constellation, it reminds us that we shine brightest together.

Inspiration:

- *Lesson:* Mend relationships and cherish togetherness.
- *Activity:* Host a family or friends' reunion, inviting everyone to share their favorite holiday memory. Write these memories on stars to hang on your tree or wall.

5. The Sleigh Bell of Kindness

Symbolism: The sleigh bell signifies the ripple effect of small acts of kindness, reminding us that generosity can echo far and wide.

Inspiration:

- *Lesson:* Look for opportunities to do good, no matter how small.
- *Activity:* Create a kindness advent calendar with your family, filling each day with small acts of kindness like baking cookies for a neighbor or donating to a local shelter.

6. The Flame of Resilience

Symbolism: The flame represents the warmth and light of resilience, the ability to keep going even in the darkest times.

Inspiration:

- *Lesson:* Find strength in adversity and share your light with others.
- *Activity:* Light a candle each night leading up to Christmas and share something you're grateful for. Reflect on challenges you've overcome this year.

7. The Crystal Compass

Symbolism: The compass symbolizes guidance, trust, and finding your path, even when the way forward is unclear.

Inspiration:

- *Lesson:* Trust your inner wisdom and seek direction in times of uncertainty.
- *Activity:* Create a vision board for the new year with your family. Include goals, dreams, and values that will guide you.

8. The Evergreen Heart

Symbolism: The Evergreen Heart reminds us of the enduring power of love and the importance of staying connected to family and friends.

Inspiration:

- *Lesson:* Love is the foundation of all holiday traditions.
- *Activity:* Write heartfelt letters to your loved ones, expressing gratitude for their presence in your life. Place these notes in stockings or under the tree.

9. The Lantern of Wisdom

Symbolism: The lantern shines a light on hidden truths and forgotten traditions, encouraging reflection and understanding.

Inspiration:

- *Lesson:* Seek wisdom in old traditions and stories.
- *Activity:* Research holiday traditions from around the world and incorporate one into your celebrations. Share what you learn with friends and family.

10. The Frost Mirror

Symbolism: The Frost Mirror reflects one's true self, challenging us to confront fears, accept flaws, and embrace growth.

Inspiration:

- *Lesson:* Growth comes from self-awareness and the courage to change.
- *Activity:* Set up a reflection corner with a mirror and write affirmations or goals for the coming year. Reflect on what you've learned about yourself this holiday season.

11. The Golden Ribbon

Symbolism: The ribbon symbolizes the ties that bind communities together and the strength found in unity.

Inspiration:

- *Lesson:* Celebrate the connections that make life meaningful.
- *Activity:* Organize a holiday potluck or community event, encouraging neighbors to come together. Use golden ribbons as part of the decorations to symbolize unity.

12. The Star of Selflessness

Symbolism: The final gift represents the culmination of all lessons, embodying the spirit of giving without expecting anything in return.

Inspiration:

- *Lesson:* True joy comes from acts of selflessness.
- *Activity:* Volunteer as a family at a local charity, or start a "pay-it-forward" chain by anonymously giving gifts or donations to those in need.

Incorporating the Lessons into Real-Life Traditions

The lessons of the Magic Calendar offer a unique opportunity to deepen your holiday traditions. Here are some additional ideas to bring these magical gifts into your celebrations:

- **Family Story Nights:** Dedicate one evening each week of December to sharing stories that reflect the themes of the Magic Calendar, such as forgiveness, hope, or generosity.
- **Magic Tokens:** Create your own version of the Magic Calendar by crafting 12 tokens, each representing a value. Draw one each day and perform an activity inspired by that value.

- **Community Spirit Tree:** Set up a tree in your town square or school and invite people to hang ornaments with wishes or acts of kindness they've performed.

By embracing the gifts of the Magic Calendar, you can turn your holiday season into a celebration of joy, connection, and the enduring magic of the human spirit.

<u>Message from the Author:</u>

I hope you enjoyed this book, I love astrology and knew there was not a book such as this out on the shelf. I love metaphysical items as well. Please check out my other books:

-Life of Government Benefits

-My life of Hell

-My life with Hydrocephalus

-Red Sky

-World Domination:Woman's rule

-World Domination:Woman's Rule 2: The War

-Life and Banishment of Apophis: book 1

-The Kidney Friendly Diet

-The Ultimate Hemp Cookbook

-Creating a Dispensary(legally)

-Cleanliness throughout life: the importance of showering from childhood to adulthood.

-Strong Roots: The Risks of Overcoddling children

-Hemp Horoscopes: Cosmic Insights and Earthly Healing

- Celestial Hemp Navigating the Zodiac: Through the Green Cosmos

-Astrological Hemp: Aligning The Stars with Earth's Ancient Herb

-The Astrological Guide to Hemp: Stars, Signs, and Sacred Leaves

-Green Growth: Innovative Marketing Strategies for your Hemp Products and Dispensary

-Cosmic Cannabis

-Astrological Munchies

-Henry The Hemp

-Zodiacal Roots: The Astrological Soul Of Hemp

- Green Constellations: Intersection of Hemp and Zodiac

-Hemp in The Houses: An astrological Adventure Through The Cannabis Galaxy

-Galactic Ganja Guide

Heavenly Hemp

Zodiac Leaves

Doctor Who Astrology

Cannastrology

Stellar Satvias and Cosmic Indicas

<u>Celestial Cannabis: A Zodiac Journey</u>

AstroHerbology: The Sky and The Soil: Volume 1

AstroHerbology:Celestial Cannabis:Volume 2

Cosmic Cannabis Cultivation

The Starry Guide to Herbal Harmony: Volume 1

The Starry Guide to Herbal Harmony: Cannabis Universe: Volume 2

Yugioh Astrology: Astrological Guide to Deck, Duels and more

Nightmare Mansion: Echoes of The Abyss

Nightmare Mansion 2: Legacy of Shadows

Nightmare Mansion 3: Shadows of the Forgotten

Nightmare Mansion 4: Echoes of the Damned

The Life and Banishment of Apophis: Book 2

Nightmare Mansion: Halls of Despair

<u>Healing with Herb: Cannabis and Hydrocephalus</u>

<u>Planetary Pot: Aligning with Astrological Herbs: Volume 1</u>

Fast Track to Freedom: 30 Days to Financial Independence Using AI, Assets, and Agile Hustles

<u>Cosmic Hemp Pathways</u>

How to Become Financially Free in 30 Days: 10,000 Paths to Prosperity

Zodiacal Herbage: Astrological Insights: Volume 1

Nightmare Mansion: Whispers in the Walls

The Daleks Invade Atlantis

Henry the hemp and Hydrocephalus

10X The Kidney Friendly Diet

Cannabis Universe: Adult coloring book

Hemp Astrology: The Healing Power of the Stars

Zodiacal Herbage: Astrological Insights: Cannabis Universe: Volume 2

<u>Planetary Pot: Aligning with Astrological Herbs: Cannabis Universes: Volume 2</u>

Doctor Who Meets the Replicators and SG-1: The Ultimate Battle for Survival

Nightmare Mansion: Curse of the Blood Moon

<u>The Celestial Stoner: A Guide to the Zodiac</u>

Cosmic Pleasures: Sex Toy Astrology for Every Sign

Hydrocephalus Astrology: Navigating the Stars and Healing Waters

Lapis and the Mischievous Chocolate Bar

Celestial Positions: Sexual Astrology for Every Sign

Apophis's Shadow Work Journal: **:** A Journey of Self-Discovery and Healing

Kinky Cosmos: Sexual Kink Astrology for Every Sign

Digital Cosmos: The Astrological Digimon Compendium

Stellar Seeds: The Cosmic Guide to Growing with Astrology

Apophis's Daily Gratitude Journal

Cat Astrology: Feline Mysteries of the Cosmos

The Cosmic Kama Sutra: An Astrological Guide to Sexual Positions

Unleash Your Potential: A Guided Journal Powered by AI Insights

Whispers of the Enchanted Grove

Cosmic Pleasures: An Astrological Guide to Sexual Kinks

369, 12 Manifestation Journal

Whisper of the nocturne journal(blank journal for writing or drawing)

The Boogey Book

Locked In Reflection: A Chastity Journey Through Locktober

Generating Wealth Quickly:

How to Generate $100,000 in 24 Hours

Star Magic: Harness the Power of the Universe

The Flatulence Chronicles: A Fart Journal for Self-Discovery

The Doctor and The Death Moth

Seize the Day: A Personal Seizure Tracking Journal

The Ultimate Boogeyman Safari: A Journey into the Boogie World and Beyond

Whispers of Samhain: 1,000 Spells of Love, Luck, and Lunar Magic: Samhain Spell Book

Apophis's guides:

Witch's Spellbook Crafting Guide for Halloween

<u>Frost & Flame: The Enchanted Yule Grimoire of 1000 Winter Spells</u>

<u>The Ultimate Boogey Goo Guide & Spooky Activities for Halloween Fun</u>

Harmony of the Scales: A Libra's Spellcraft for Balance and Beauty

The Enchanted Advent: 36 Days of Christmas Wonders

Nightmare Mansion: The Labyrinth of Screams

Harvest of Enchantment: 1,000 Spells of Gratitude, Love, and Fortune for Thanksgiving

The Boogey Chronicles: A Journal of Nightly Encounters and Shadowy Secrets

The 12 Days of Financial Freedom: A Step-by-Step Christmas Countdown to Transform Your Finances

Sigil of the Eternal Spiral Blank Journal

A Christmas Feast: Timeless Recipes for Every Meal

Holiday Stress-Free Solutions: A Survival Guide to Thriving During the Festive Season

Yu-Gi-Oh! Holiday Gifting Mastery: The Ultimate Guide for Fans and Newcomers Alike

Holiday Harmony: A Hydrocephalus Survival Guide for the Festive Season

Celestial Craft: The Witch's Almanac for 2025 – A Cosmic Guide to Manifestations, Moons, and Mystical Events

Doctor Who: The Toymaker's Winter Wonderland

Tulsa King Unveiled: A Thrilling Guide to Stallone's Mafia Masterpiece

Pendulum Craft: A Complete Guide to Crafting and Using Personalized Divination Tools

Nightmare Mansion: Santa's Eternal Eve

Starlight Noel: A Cosmic Journey through Christmas Mysteries

The Dark Architect: Unlocking the Blueprint of Existence

Surviving the Embrace: The Ultimate Guide to Encounters with The Hugging Molly

The Enchanted Codex: Secrets of the Craft for Witches, Wiccans, and Pagans

Harvest of Gratitude: A Complete Thanksgiving Guide

Yuletide Essentials: A Complete Guide to an Authentic and Magical Christmas

Celestial Smokes: A Cosmic Guide to Cigars and Astrology

Living in Balance: A Comprehensive Survival Guide to Thriving with Diabetes Insipidus

Cosmic Symbiosis: The Venom Zodiac Chronicles

The Cursed Paw of Ambition

Cosmic Symbiosis: The Astrological Venom Journal

Celestial Wonders Unfold: A Stargazer's Guide to the Cosmos (2024-2029)

The Ultimate Black Friday Prepper's Guide: Mastering Shopping Strategies and Savings

Cosmic Sales: The Astrological Guide to Black Friday Shopping

Legends of the Corn Mother and Other Harvest Myths

Whispers of the Harvest: The Corn Mother's Journal

The Evergreen Spellbook

The Doctor Meets the Boogeyman

The White Witch of Rose Hall's SpellBook

The Gingerbread Golem's Shadow: A Study in Sweet Darkness

The Gingerbread Golem Codex: An Academic Exploration of Sweet Myths

The Gingerbread Golem Grimoire: Sweet Magicks and Spells for the Festive Witch

The Curse of the Gingerbread Golem

10-minute Christmas Crafts for kids

<u>Christmas Crisis Solutions: The Ultimate Last-Minute Survival Guide</u>

Gingerbread Golem Recipes: Holiday Treats with a Magical Twist

The Infinite Key: Unlocking Mystical Secrets of the Ages

Enchanted Yule: A Wiccan and Pagan Guide to a Magical and Memorable Season

Dinosaurs of Power: Unlocking Ancient Magick

Astro-Dinos: The Cosmic Guide to Prehistoric Wisdom

Gallifrey's Yule Logs: A Festive Doctor Who Cookbook

The Dino Grimoire: Secrets of Prehistoric Magick

The Gift They Never Knew They Needed

The Gingerbread Golem's Culinary Alchemy: Enchanting Recipes for a Sweetly Dark Feast

A Time Lord Christmas: Holiday Adventures with the Doctor

Krampusproofing Your Home: Defensive Strategies for Yule

Silent Frights: A Collection of Christmas Creepypastas to Chill Your Bones

Santa Raptor's Jolly Carnage: A Dino-Claus Christmas Tale

Prehistoric Palettes: A Dino Wicca Coloring Journey

The Christmas Wishkeeper Chronicles

The Starlight Sleigh: A Holiday Journey

Elf Secrets: The True Magic of the North Pole

Candy Cane Conjurations

Cooking with Kids: Recipes Under 20 Minutes

Doctor Who: The TARDIS Confiscation

The Anxiety First Aid Kit: Quick Tools to Calm Your Mind

Frosty Whispers: A Winter's Tale

The Infinite Key: Unlocking the Secrets to Prosperity, Resilience, and Purpose

The Grasping Void: Why You'll Regret This Purchase

Astrology for Busy Bees: Star Signs Simplified

The Instant Focus Formula: Cut Through the Noise

The Secret Language of Colors: Unlocking the Emotional Codes

Sacred Fossil Chronicles: Blank Journal

The Christmas Cottage Miracle

Feeding Frenzy: Graboid-Inspired Recipes

Manifest in Minutes: The Quick Law of Attraction Guide

The Symbiote Chronicles: Doctor Who's Venomous Journey

Think Tiny, Grow Big: The Minimalist Mindset

The Energy Key: Unlocking Limitless Motivation

New Year, New Magic: Manifesting Your Best Year Yet

Unstoppable You: Mastering Confidence in Minutes

Infinite Energy: The Secret to Never Feeling Drained

Lightning Focus: Mastering the Art of Productivity in a Distracted World

Saturnalia Manifestation Magick: A Guide to Unlocking Abundance During the Solstice

Graboids and Garland: The Ultimate Tremors-Themed Christmas Guide

If you want solar for your home go here: https://www.harborso-lar.live/apophisenterprises/

Get Some Tarot cards: https://www.makeplayingcards.com/sell/apophis-occult-shop

Get some shirts: https://www.bonfire.com/store/apophis-shirt-emporium/

<u>**Instagrams:**</u>
@apophis_enterprises,
@apophisbookemporium,
@apophisscardshop
Twitter: @apophisenterpr1
 Tiktok:@apophisenterprise
Youtube: @sg1fan23477, @FiresideRetreatKingdom
Hive: @sg1fan23477
CheeLee: @SG1fan23477

Podcast: Apophis Chat Zone: https://open.spotify.com/show/
5zXbrCLEV2xzCp8ybrfHsk?si=fb4d4fdbdce44dec

Newsletter: https://apophiss-newsletter-27c897.beehiiv.com/

If you want to support me or see posts of other projects that I have come over to: **buymeacoffee.com/mpetchinskg**
I post there daily several times a day

Get your Dinowicca or Christmas themed digital products, especially Santa Raptor songs and other musics. Here: **https://sg1fan23477.gumroad.com**

Apophis Yuletide Digital has not only digital Christmas items, but it will have all things with Dinowicca as well as other Digital products.